THE LITTLE
BOOK OF

# CATS

Happy Birthday

purr, purr, meow, meep

Sooty, Bugsy
Bubbles &
Friend.

What do cats read
every morning?
Mewspapers

What do cats
strive for?

# Pur-r-rfection

What's the name of
your kitten?
I don't know, it
won't tell me.

What kind of exercise
do cats like most?
Puss-ups

When is it unlucky to see
a black cat?
When you're a mouse.

What do cats eat
for breakfast?
Mewsli

# CAT
# JOKES

or give it a good
stroke right under
its chin.

PUR-R-R-R

And if your cat's older,

find it a comfy place
for a good catnap...

a piece of paper, a toy mouse, or a ball of wool...

# A ball...

Cats and kittens love
to play. Just give
them something that
moves and they're off
and away.

# TIME TO PLAY

When your cat's all clean and shiny, give it a smart collar with your name and number. Now you can be sure it will always find its way home.

Don't worry about baths
unless your cat has extra
long hair. Then take it
regularly to be properly
coiffed.

Brush daily to give your cat a clean, shiny coat and to avoid nasty matting or knotting.

And cats like to nap in
the sun – sixteen hours
a day! When your
cat licks its fur clean,
just think of all the
vitamin D it will glean.

Cats bathe themselves
every day.

# GROOMING
# YOUR CAT

If your cat's on
the chubby side, you
can bet it's
been getting a
titbit or two
on the sly!

...so be proud when
your cat brings home
its first delicious bird
or mouse dinner.

*Yum, yum!*

Well-fed cats stick close to home; peckish cats hunt far and wide.

Meat is a staple in every cat's diet...

Milk is a welcome treat,
but too much will upset
your cat's tummy.

Cats love their food,
canned or dry. Feed
them at the
same time every
day, and
give them
plenty of
water too.

# FEEDING YOUR CAT

or you want your cat
to be snug and cuddly
ALL the time.

you want to train
your cat to sit,
stay and fetch...

A cat's for you unless...

you have a big dog
who's head of the roost...

# it's up to you to choose!

A hairy cat or a bald
cat, a pedigree cat or a
moggy? Cats come in
all shapes and sizes –

# CHOOSING
## A CAT

Old Snowbie, the
longest cat in the world,
measures 1.03 metres
(3 ft 4 1/2 in) from nose
to tail, and lives
in Aberdeenshire.

Towser, who lives in Scotland, is the best mouser in the world. He's caught over 28,899 mice – an average of three a day.

Tom, a black and white cat, stowed away in the hold of a BA jet and flew half a million miles in two months. Among its stopovers were Australia, Jamaica and Kuwait – not bad for a cat.

The largest litter?
A four-year-old cat had
nineteen kittens in 1970.

The greenest cat in the
world was born in
Denmark in 1996.
Yes, its fur is green!

# Amazing Cat Facts

and fiendishly
aloof cats.

Wherever they are at,
cats are what I truly love...

singing-on-the-roof cats,

sad cats,

mad cats,

**bad**

cats,

# glad

cats,

little-ball-of-
fluff cats,

Tough cats,

rough cats,

cats...

like her!

cats that cuddle,

PUR-R-R-R-R-R-R

and cats that purr,

# Cats that preen

or sitting-on-
a-mat cats.

scooting-through-
the-flap cats,

and very
nearly flat cats,

fabulously

**fat**

cats,

prim cats,

posey cats,

Dippy, trippy, dozy cats,

sugar~white,

tabby,

tiger-striped,

spotty,

cats asleep,

cats that hunt,

cats that

leap,

Cats that linger,

prinking cats,

thinking cats.

licking,
lapping,
drinking
cats,

hissing
cats,

HISS

HISS

mean cats,

kissing cats,

Keen cats,

round a bin,

in your socks!

on a broom,

in a box,

on a knee,      through a gap,

up a tree,          on your lap,

streaking up a stair,

stalking down
a butterfly,

cats in bags,

cats in coats,

cats in rags,

cats in collars,

round cats,

square cats,

found cats,

Lost cats,

proud

cats.

# scared

cats,

Howling,
yowling,
rowdy cats,

cute cats...

...lazy cats.

crazy
cats,

Tatty,

scatty,

and **play,**

cats that sit in
the sun all day.

Cats that **bounce**

and

**pounce**

lurking-near-the-hob cats –
any one would do!

bobcats,

bald cats,

slob cats,

Clean cats,

groovy, ravy, stray cats.

stay-at-home-tame cats,

royal cats,

# dozy

cats,

loyal cats,

# happy

cats,

**many**

cats,

# skinny

cats,

# roly-poly

mum cats,

pretty little kitty cats,

# Big,
## rough
tomcats,

Don't you like them too?

nosy cats –

# cosy

cats,

bold

cats,

shy cats,

Soppy,
floppy,
old cats,

Wherever I go,
I look for cats —
cats are my
favourite things.

# THE LITTLE
# BOOK OF
# CATS

Judy Hindley and
Margaret Chamberlain

RED
FOX

A Red Fox Book

Published by Random House Children's Books
20 Vauxhall Bridge Road, London SW1V 2SA

A division of The Random House Group Ltd
London Melbourne Sydney Auckland
Johannesburg and agencies throughout the world

Text copyright © Judy Hindley 2000
Illustrations copyright © Margaret Chamberlain 2000

1 3 5 7 9 10 8 6 4 2

First published in Great Britain by Red Fox 2000

Printed in China

THE RANDOM HOUSE GROUP Limited Reg. No. 954009
www.randomhouse.co.uk

ISBN 0 09 940914 3